Flowertot
Rainbow

Created by Keith Chapman

First published in Great Britain by HarperCollins Children's Books in 2006

1 3 5 7 9 10 8 6 4 2
ISBN-13: 978-0-00-722319-0
ISBN-10: 0-00-722319-6

Based on the television series *Fifi and the Flowertots* and the
original script 'Flowertot Rainbow' by Diane Redmond
© Chapman Entertainment Limited 2006

Printed and bound in China

Flowertot Rainbow

HarperCollins *Children's Books*

Fifi Forget-Me-Not was very happy. Violet had painted her a beautiful picture.

"You're sooo clever, Violet." Fifi said.
"You're always giving me pretty things."
"That's because you're my friend, Fifi,"
Violet said sweetly.
She loved making presents for her
friends and was the best painter
in Flowertot Garden.
"Well, I'm going to give you something,"
Fifi decided. "What would you like?"
Violet thought for a moment.
"Colours!" she said, throwing her arms
up in the air. "Colours are my favourite
thing in all the world!"
"Colours?" thought Fifi.
"Hmm, I wonder..."

Back in Forget-Me-Not Cottage, Fifi shared her plan with Bumble. "I'm going to give Violet a big colour surprise!" Fifi giggled, pointing to a row of shoots in her flowerbed. Bumble nodded. "You said the seeds will grow into red and yellow and pink and orange and purple and blue flowers!"

"They will if I give them plenty of water and the sun keeps on shining!" Fifi said as she gently watered all of the shoots. "Then I pick a big bunch of flowers, all the colours of the rainbow, and give them to Violet!"

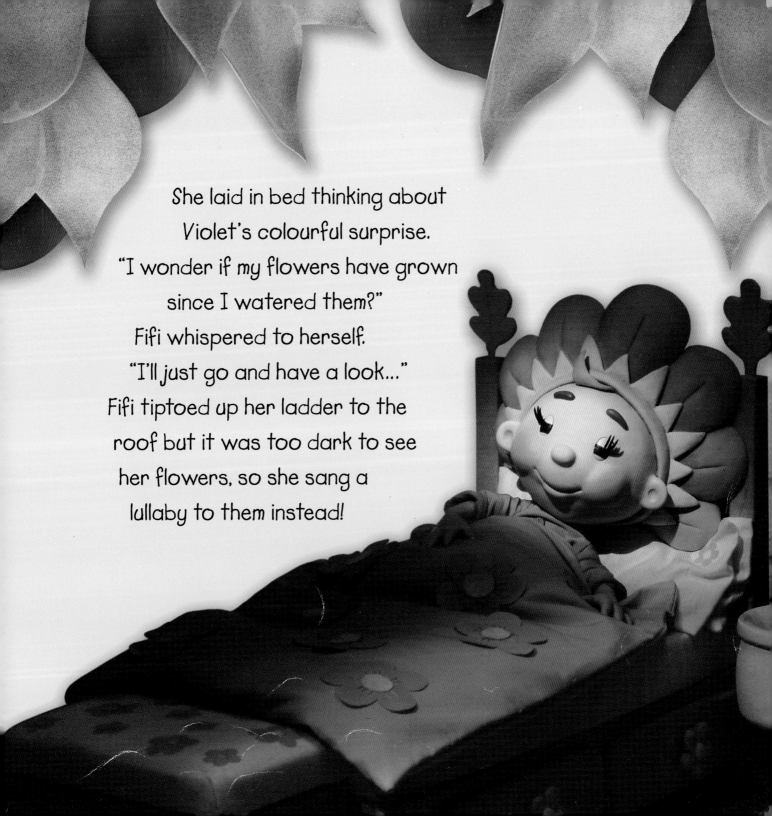

She laid in bed thinking about
Violet's colourful surprise.
"I wonder if my flowers have grown
since I watered them?"
Fifi whispered to herself.
"I'll just go and have a look..."
Fifi tiptoed up her ladder to the
roof but it was too dark to see
her flowers, so she sang a
lullaby to them instead!

The next morning, Fifi dashed out to see her flowers as soon as the sun was up.
"You're still wearing your pyjamas, Fifi!" came a laughing voice from across the garden.
It was Bumble.
"I forgot to change into my... oh Fiddly Flowerpetals, I've forgotten!"
Fifi burst into a great big chuckle.
"Ha ha, Fifi Forget-Me-Not forgot!"
Bumble teased.
"You mean your dungarees."

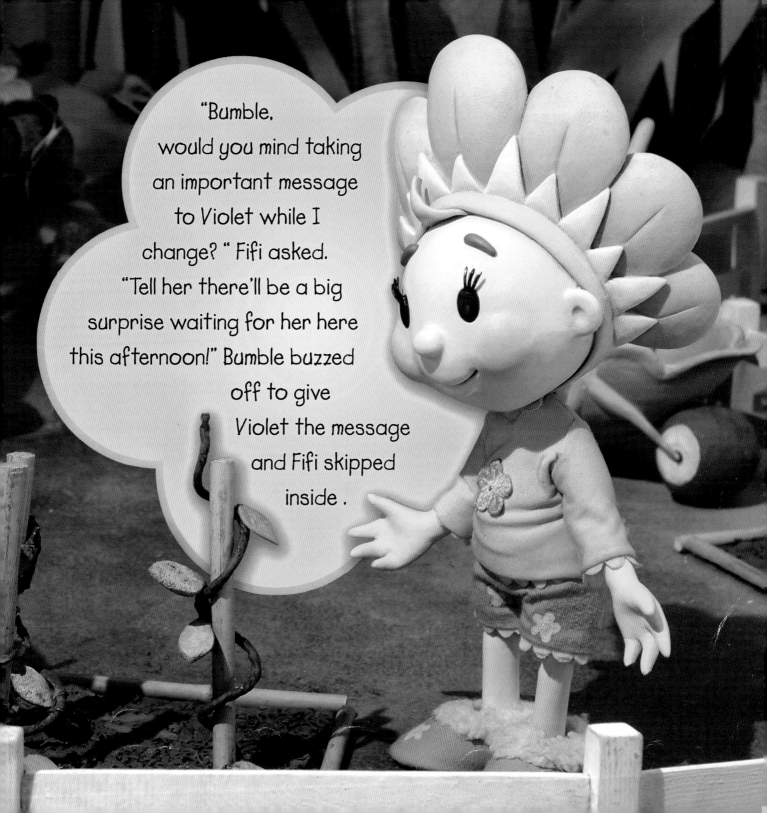

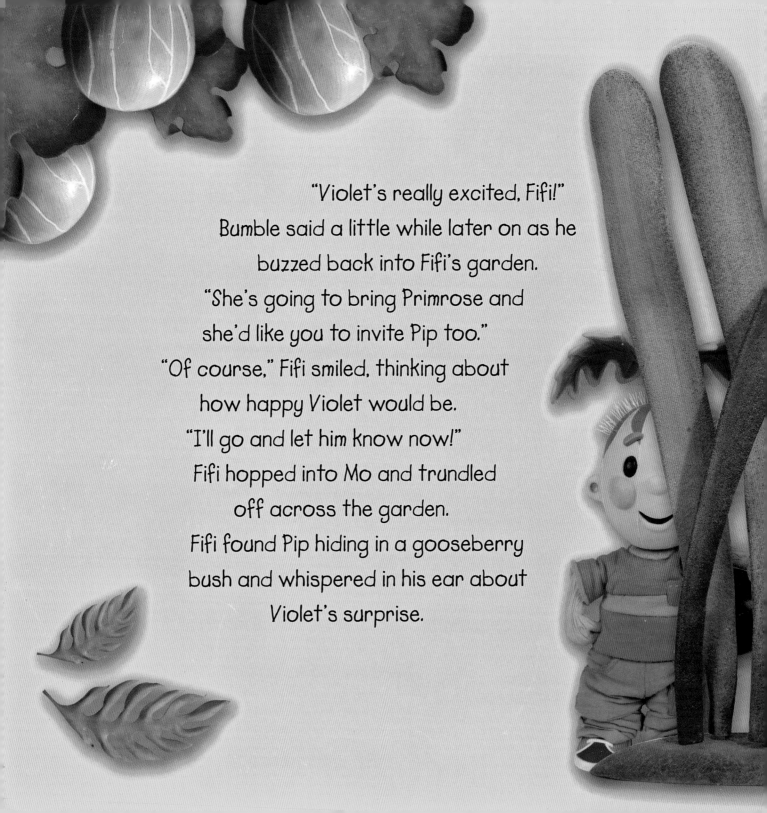

"Violet's really excited, Fifi!"
Bumble said a little while later on as he
buzzed back into Fifi's garden.
"She's going to bring Primrose and
she'd like you to invite Pip too."
"Of course," Fifi smiled, thinking about
how happy Violet would be.
"I'll go and let him know now!"
Fifi hopped into Mo and trundled
off across the garden.
Fifi found Pip hiding in a gooseberry
bush and whispered in his ear about
Violet's surprise.

"I'd love to
see Violet's surprise!"
he cried.
"But can we play hide
and seek first? You cover
your eyes and count to ten."
"Oh alright," Fifi said, "just a quick game.
1, 2, 3, 4..."
But before Fifi could even
get to five, Pip was
already
hiding!

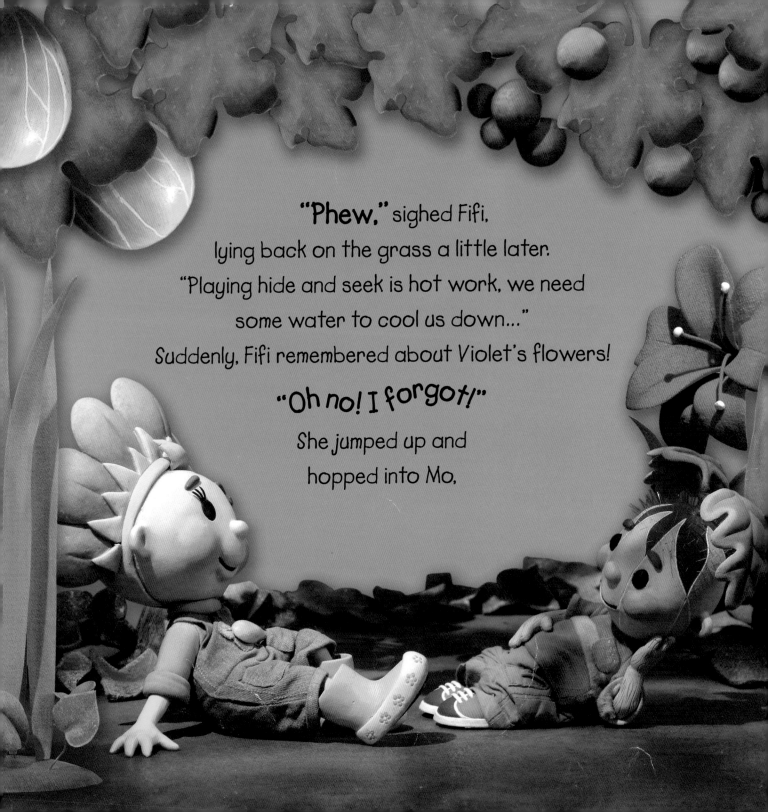

"Phew," sighed Fifi,
lying back on the grass a little later.
"Playing hide and seek is hot work, we need
some water to cool us down..."
Suddenly, Fifi remembered about Violet's flowers!

"Oh no! I forgot!"

She jumped up and
hopped into Mo,

Back in her garden,
Fifi's flowerbed was a very
sorry sight. The flowers had all drooped
because they were too hot.
"Violet's going to be sooo disappointed,"
Bumble muttered as he buzzed down.
"Buttercups and Daisies," Fifi cried,
"what am I going to give Violet?"
But before anyone could suggest anything,
a raindrop plopped into the flowerbed.
Fifi looked up at the
darkening sky.
"A thunderstorm!
Quickly, get under cover."

Soon the thunder stopped and Fifi saw a beautiful rainbow spreading across the sky! Before she could show anyone, Violet and Primrose skipped into the garden.

"Bumble told us you had a
big surprise for Violet,"
Primrose said,
a tad bossily.

Fifi nodded and smiled mysteriously. "I have! There you are Violet." she said, pointing to the rainbow. "A sky full of colour just for you!"

"Oh, Fifi, it's beautiful!" said Violet.

Violet gave Fifi a
great big hug and a kiss
on the cheek, while the other
Flowertots were
admiring the rainbow.

Bumble noticed
that Fifi's flowers had
all grown again!
"Must have been all that rain!"
thought Bumble as he
quietly began
picking a huge bunch.

"I picked these for
you to give to Violet,"
Bumble winked at his forgetful
friend and handed over the biggest
bunch of flowers Fifi had ever seen.
"What would I do without
you, Bumble?"
Fifi smiled.

The Flowertots all
gathered round to admire
the pretty flowers.
"Thank you for my rainbow
in the sky and my rainbow
in your garden!"
Violet said, delighted.
"Two beautiful rainbows
from my friend, Fifi!"

Make Your Own Flowertot Rainbow

This is a quick and fun way to grow lots of brightly coloured flowers.

You will need: * A bunch of white flowers * Scissors * Food colouring in your favourite colours * Vases * A ribbon

1. First, ask a grown-up to cut the bottom two centimetres off the end of the flower stalks.

2. Now fill each vase half full with water and add a few drops of your favourite food colouring.

3. Now pop your cut flowers in to the vases and leave them on a bright sunny windowsill for a couple of days.

4. If you watch carefully, you'll see the petals of the flowers start to change colour!

5. Once your flowers have bloomed and taken on the colour of the food colouring, tie them with a pretty ribbon and give them to someone special.

Remember, the more food colouring you add, the darker the colours will be.